HarperCollinsPublishers

Who'll Pull Santa's Sleigh Tonight?

Laura Rader

Christmas was just around the corner.
The toys were wrapped. The lists were checked.
Santa's sleigh was polished and ready to go.
"Let's visit the reindeer," said Santa to Mrs. Claus.

As they approached the stable, Santa called out:
"Hello, Dasher, Dancer, Prancer, and Vixen!
Hello, Comet, Cupid, Donder, and Blitzen!
Are you ready to fly?"

The answer was a loud . . .

Ahh-CHOO!!

"Goodness gracious!" exclaimed Mrs. Claus.
The reindeer looked miserable.

"We aw hab codes!" said Dancer.
"Poor deer!" said Mrs. Claus.

Santa rushed off to tell the elves.
"The reindeer are sick!
Who'll pull the sleigh?!" he asked.
"We need a backup plan."

Santa paced up and down.
He scratched his head and looked serious.

Then he had an idea. "We'll find stand-ins!" he said.

The auditions were announced.
A large crowd lined up to try out.

ACTION!!

The performers were very unusual.

The Winged Monkeys

The Amazing Mc Quacks

The Fly-Away Hares

So were their acts.

The Happy Hoofers

Next!

None was right for the job.

Poor Santa.

Santa went to his workshop.
He thought. He sketched.
He thought some more.
Then he had an idea!

"Here's my new plan!" said Santa.

There were a few grumbles and groans.
But Santa and the elves went to work.

They worked hard. They worked fast.
At last they finished.
"We did it!" shouted Santa. "Let's show Mrs. Claus!"

It was the **BIGGEST** idea Santa had ever had!

Santa prepared for a test flight.

The balloon went up, up, up.

The balloon was deflated. So was Santa.

"I'm all out of ideas," he sighed.

"I'll bring you a cup of hot cocoa," said Mrs. Claus.

Santa sipped the cocoa.
"Ahhh!" he said. "This always
makes me feel good as new."
Santa and Mrs. Claus looked
at each other.
I have an idea," said Santa.
"Do you think . . . ?"

"Yes! I DO!" she finished.

Santa and Mrs. Claus took a big
pot of cocoa to the reindeer.
"I hope this works," said Santa.

The reindeer stopped sniffling.
They stopped sneezing.
They looked *much* better.
They were ready to fly!
"Hot cocoa saved the day!" Mrs. Claus said.

Everyone cheered as they flew out of sight.

Hot cocoa for all and

to all a good night!

This is delicious!

Ask an adult to help you!

Santa's Special Hot Cocoa

Makes 3 delicious mugs!

INGREDIENTS
2 Tbsp. cocoa
3 Tbsp. sugar
¼ cup hot water
1½ cups milk
a lot of tiny marshmallows (optional)
3 candy canes (optional)

Pour cocoa and sugar into a saucepan and slowly add hot water. Stir until ingredients are blended together. Bring mixture to a boil. Boil over medium heat for about 2 minutes, stirring constantly. Reduce heat and add milk, stirring occasionally, until entire mixture is heated thoroughly. DO NOT BOIL. Remove from heat and stir well. If you want, serve with marshmallows and candy canes. Add a big dash of Christmas cheer (for the best flavor)!

For my mother, who knew Santa very well.
With love, L. R.

Mmmm!

Who'll Pull Santa's Sleigh Tonight?

Copyright © 2003 by Laura Rader   Manufactured in China.   All rights reserved.
www.harperchildrens.com

Library of Congress Cataloging-in-Publication Data
Rader, Laura.
Who'll pull Santa's sleigh tonight? / Laura Rader.— 1st ed.   p. cm.
Summary: When the reindeer get bad colds, Santa Claus wonders who will be able to pull his
sleigh on Christmas Eve.   ISBN 0-06-008088-4 — ISBN 0-06-008089-2 (lib. bdg.)
[1. Santa Claus—Fiction. 2. Reindeer—Fiction. 3. Sick—Fiction.] I. Title.
PZ7.R1155 Wh 2003   [E]—dc21   2002012739   CIP   AC

Typography by Carla Weise
1 2 3 4 5 6 7 8 9 10
❖
First Edition